The LONG, LONG LETTER

Elizabeth Spurr   Illustrated by David Catrow

Hyperion Paperbacks for Children
New York

$\mathcal{M}$y mother got a postcard from Aunt Hetta. It read: *Sister dear, don't you owe me a letter?*

She received a second message: *I've had no mail for a dog's age!*

A third—in bold calligraphy— said:
Have you quite forgotten me?

"Land o' lovin'," sighed my mother. "Why, just last month I wrote her. Poor woman must be lonely, way out there in the boonies. With no kith nor kin to care for, she has too much time to fret. I'd better write a long, long letter—one she will *not* forget!"

My mother sat down at her pine-topped desk to write. With a fine plumed pen she looped and scrolled, morning, noon, and into night. She badly burned the dinner. It was a long, long letter.

She wrote through fall and winter, into spring and summer. The days grew warmer, longer. I grew taller, stronger. It was a long, long letter.

She wrote of cabbages and crocuses, sausages and shoes. The newly born, the price of corn, the cranking phone she'd never use.

Of darning socks and scouring pots, broken clocks and knitting knots. She wrote of all the chores she had no time to do—thanks to the long, long letter.

One day after breakfast she said, "Let us mail the letter. There's still so much to tell her, but I've no more ink nor paper."

We put the letter into boxes and hauled it in a wagon. We gave it to the postman, who stuck a thousand stamps on. It *was* a long, long letter.

On the way to the train station a whirlwind came from nowhere. It whipped the tops right off the boxes. *Swoosh!* went Aunt Hetta's letter. *Whoosh!* The pages scattered. It was an all-gone letter.

Aunt Hetta lived a crooked mile from the town of Neverbee. The townsfolk rarely passed her way, much less passed the time of day with tea and friendly chatter. And none had sent a cheery word by way of card or letter. She was a lone, lone Hetta.

By her mailbox sat Aunt Hetta. She sat in her carved rocker, with a pocketful of crackers and a pot of peanut butter. She rocked and watched around the clock from Monday until Sunday—waiting for the pleasure of a letter from my mother.

She rocked in fall and winter, through the spring and summer. The days again grew shorter, but there was no long, long letter. She pleaded with the post-man, "Just a small one or a thin one?" How she longed, longed, longed for *any* letter.

She ate peanut-buttered crackers to kill the pangs of hunger, but her heart still ached and hungered for a letter. Where *was* the missive from her sister? How could it have missed her? She'd kept a hawk's watch on the mailbox since a year ago September!

December's storm clouds gathered. Aunt Hetta
watched and shivered. The wind howled loud
and bitter. The dark skies dumped a blizzard.

It was the *wrong, wrong* weather to sit waiting
for a letter.

In her fringed shawl Hetta huddled, bone-
chilled and befuddled. White flakes danced
around her; soon all was covered over. Mailbox.
Rocker. Peanut butter. And, of course, Aunt
Hetta.

All was silent. All was still. Then slowly, from a whitened hill, peeked the head of—yes—Aunt Hetta. She was beaming like the sun and staring cross-eyed at **her letter!**

One evening over tea my mother read to me a fat, fat letter from Aunt Hetta:

You might say that I have been a bit under the weather. I thought it was a snowstorm. But it was your "airmail" letter!

Such a long, long letter. The town was in a dither. It took three days to gather, with snowplows and a tractor.

I am told that 'midst the rumpus the postman said, "Great Zeus's thunder! What's become of Hetta Pinkus? She was sitting by her mailbox. She must be six feet under!"

Through the vineyards, through the groves, the townsfolk rushed in droves. Headed by the doctor—and followed by the preacher—a posse for emergency was coming out to rescue me!

Plain to see, ca-tas-tro-phe draws good folks together. I felt like a ce-leb-ri-ty, instead of a non-entity. Life looked a lot, lot brighter!

I said, "Thank you!" to the rescue team. "Your concern is flattering. But I've suffered no great harm. My sister's letter kept me warm."

As the townsfolk shoveled, the postman winked and chuckled, "That's what I'd call writing up a storm!"

Fifty children stacked the pages (you forgot to number).
They piled them in the haymow, stored them in the silo. They
filled the springhouse and the mill, the granary and the still. It
was a long, long letter.

I planned to sit down with your letter, catch up on the news.
But in the dis-com-bob-u-la-tion of my recent situation, I have
lost my spectacles.

I cannot read your long, long letter!
Fifty children have been rummaging through attic, house, and cellar, looking for my glasses. But perhaps it doesn't matter . . .

. . . *for now I have* **one hundred eyes**! *But, best of all, I re-al-ize this town is filled with caring friends. I'll never feel alone again—*
thanks to your long, long letter.

First Hyperion Paperback edition 1997

Text ©1996 by Elizabeth Spurr.
Illustrations © 1996 by David Catrow.

A hardcover edition of *The Long, Long Letter* is available from
Hyperion Books for Children.

Printed in Hong Kong by South China Printing Company (1988) Ltd.

3 5 7 9 10 8 6 4

Library of Congress Cataloging-in-Publication Data
Spurr, Elizabeth
The long, long letter/Elizabeth Spurr; illustrated by David Catrow—1st
Hyperion Books for Children ed.
p.   cm.
Summary: Mother's long, long letter brings Aunt Hetta surprise and
adventure, as the loose pages bury her house and keep her warm during
the winter.
ISBN 0-7868-0127-1 (trade)—ISBN 0-7868-2100-0 (lib. bdg.)
—ISBN 0-7868-1202-8 (pbk.)
[1. Letters—fiction. 2. Aunts—fiction. 3. Tall tales.]
I. Catrow, David, ill. II. Title
PZ7.S7695Lo 1996
[E]—dc 20
95-8073

The artwork for this book is prepared using watercolors.
The text for this book is set in 18-point Weiss.

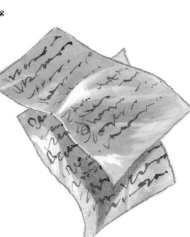